33x   11/07 4/08
35x 9/09 ✓ 11/09
35x 11/09 1/10
39x 3/12 ✓ 4/12
40x 12/13 ✓ 7/14

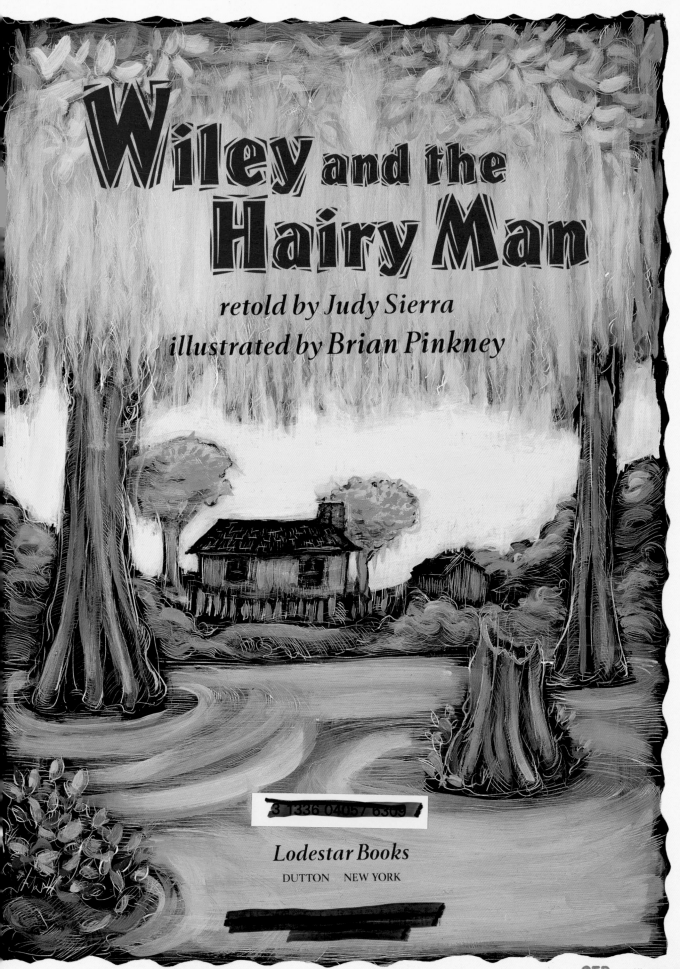

Wiley and the Hairy Man

retold by *Judy Sierra*

illustrated by *Brian Pinkney*

Lodestar Books

DUTTON   NEW YORK

Library of Congress Cataloging-in-Publication Data
Sierra, Judy.
Wiley and the Hairy Man / retold by Judy Sierra;
illustrated by Brian Pinkney.—1st ed.
p.   cm.
Summary: With his mother's help, Wiley outwits the
conjuring Hairy Man that lives in the swamp
near their home
ISBN 0—525—67477—2
[1. Afro—Americans—Folklore.   2. Folklore—United States]
I. Pinkney, Brian, ill.   II. Title.
PZ8.1.S573Wi   1996
398.2'089'96073—dc20
94—24512
CIP   AC

Published in the United States by Lodestar Books,
an affiliate of Dutton Children's Books,
a division of Penguin Books USA Inc.,
375 Hudson Street, New York, New York 10014

Published simultaneously in Canada
by McClelland & Stewart, Toronto
Editor: Virginia Buckley   Designer: Marilyn Granald
Printed in Hong Kong   First Edition
10 9 8 7 6 5 4 3 2 1

to Bob, because he loves telling this story
J.S.

to my brother-in-law Leon, a good Hairy Man
B.P.

A boy named Wiley lived with his mama in a cabin down by the edge of the swamp. One cold night, Wiley's daddy fell off the ferryboat, and no one could find hide nor hair of him afterward. Folks whispered that the Hairy Man must have carried him off. Then they heard someone laughing way back in the trees. "That's the Hairy Man for sure," folks agreed, and they stopped looking for Wiley's daddy.

"You be careful, Wiley," said Wiley's mama. "The Hairy Man got your daddy, and he'll get you, too, if you don't watch out."

"Don't worry, Mama," Wiley said. "I'll take my hound dogs everywhere I go. That Hairy Man can't stand hound dogs."

Wiley's mama smiled because she knew that was true. Wiley's mama knew lots of things, like conjure magic.

One day, Wiley went out to gather kindling wood, and he left his hound dogs tied up on the porch. He couldn't find much wood, so he kept walking deeper and deeper into the swamp. Everything was still and quiet, and Wiley felt a chill climb up the back of his neck. He turned around real quick and saw a man coming toward him through the trees, grinning. The man sure was ugly, and that grin didn't help much. He was hairy all over, and his eyes glowed red.

"Hello, Wiley," the man said.

"Don't you look at me like that, Mister Hairy Man," said Wiley. He glanced down and saw that the Hairy Man didn't have feet like a person. He had feet like a cow. Now, Wiley reckoned he had never seen a cow up a tree, so straightaway he shimmied up the nearest bay tree.

"You come down here, Wiley!" shouted the Hairy Man.

"You come up and get me," Wiley shouted back.

The Hairy Man just grinned, and drool rolled off his long, yellow teeth. "No thank you, Wiley. I'll just wait right here till you get tired or hungry."

Wiley thought about that Hairy Man down there on the ground, and he thought about his hound dogs back home, and he came up with a plan.

"Mister Hairy Man, I hear you know conjure magic."

"Why, I'm the best conjure man in the county," the Hairy Man boasted.

"I'll bet you can't make something just disappear," said Wiley.

"Something like that bird's nest sitting there at the end of the branch?" the Hairy Man asked. "Now it's disappeared!"

Wiley looked at the empty branch. "Well, how do I know that bird's nest was there in the first place? I'll bet you can't make something I know is there disappear."

"Heh, heh," chuckled the Hairy Man. "Where's your shirt?"

Wiley looked down, and his shirt was gone.

"Aw, that was just a plain ordinary everyday shirt," Wiley said. "But I'll bet you can't make this disappear." And he pointed to the rope that was holding up his britches. "This rope is special because my mama used conjure on it. No one can make my mama's magic conjure rope disappear."

"Shucks, I can make every single piece of rope in this county disappear." Then the Hairy Man roared out, "Every rope in this here county has done disappeared!"

Wiley held tight to his britches to keep them from falling down, and he laughed because the Hairy Man had done just what he wanted him to do. "Yessir, you are a mighty good conjure man," said Wiley. He took a big, deep breath and called out, "Here dogs! Here dogs! Here dogs!"

There was a sound of hound dogs yelping and barking, coming closer and closer. That old Hairy Man took off into the swamp lickety-split. Wiley ran on home and told his mama what had happened.

"Wiley," she said, "you fooled the Hairy Man one time, and that's good. If you can fool him twice more, he'll be bound to stay away from you for good and forever."

"I hope I never see him again, with that ugly hair and slobbering grin."

"Tell me, Wiley, was he carrying a sack?" Wiley's mama asked.

"Yes, ma'am. A big croaker sack."

Wiley's mama smiled. "I just thought of a way for you to put the Hairy Man in the dirt."

"If I put him in the dirt, he'll put me in his croaker sack."

"Listen to me," said his mama. "Go into the swamp tomorrow, and leave your dogs here at home. When you see the Hairy Man, tell him he can't change himself into some great big animal. If you say he can't do something, he'll do it for sure. Then tell him he can't turn into some small, slow animal, and he'll do that, too. And when he does, shove that Hairy Man slam-bang into the croaker sack."

"Then I can toss him into the river with the croaker fish," laughed Wiley.

The next morning, Wiley shut his dogs in the cabin and walked off toward the swamp, whistling all the while to keep up his courage. He hadn't gone far when he got that same creepy feeling on the back of his neck. The next instant, the Hairy Man stepped from behind a tree and stood right in front of him.

"Hello there, Wiley."

"Hello, Hairy Man," said Wiley. "What have you got in that croaker sack?"

"I ain't got nothin' *yet* Wiley," the Hairy Man grunted, and he laid the sack down on the ground next to him.

"Mister Hairy Man," Wiley said, "I hear tell you can change yourself into any animal you want."

"You heard right," said the Hairy Man, and he was grinning real big and drooling something fierce.

"You can't change into a great big animal like a bear," said Wiley.

The Hairy Man spun around, and there stood a huge, hairy bear, and that bear was just smiling and drooling and looking straight at Wiley.

"Tha-that's pretty g-good," said Wiley, "but you can't change into an alligator."

The bear whirled around, and two seconds later, Wiley was staring straight down into an alligator's mouth full of slobbery, yellow teeth.

"You s-sure are a g-good conjure man," said Wiley, "but you can't change yourself into a little bitty baby possum."

The alligator twisted and turned, and when the dust settled, there was a tiny possum crawling in the dirt. Wiley grabbed the possum and slammed it into the croaker sack. He tied it up real tight and went and threw it into the river.

Wiley started off home, feeling mighty proud of himself.
But then he heard the Hairy Man's voice rising up out of the
swamp.

"Wiley! W-i-i-i-i-ley! I'm a-coming to get you . . . *tonight!*"

Wiley ran as fast as his legs could carry him. "I did exactly what you said," he told his mama, "but the Hairy Man got out of the sack, and he says he's coming here tonight to get me."

"Why, that Hairy Man must have conjured up the wind to blow him out of that sack," said Wiley's mama. "But still, you did fool him a second time." Then she sat in her rocking chair and rocked and studied how they could play the Hairy Man one more trick.

In the meantime, Wiley ran around and did everything he could think of to keep the Hairy Man from coming inside the cabin. He tied up one of his hound dogs on the front porch, and one out back. He closed the shutters and set up a broom handle across the window because no evil thing can step over a broom handle. He built a big fire in the fireplace in case the Hairy Man had a mind to come down the chimney.

Finally his mama stopped rocking and said, "Run out to the barn, Wiley, and bring me back one of those newborn baby pigs."

As Wiley was going to the barn, a peculiar animal, sort of like a boar only twice as big, ran by. One of Wiley's hound dogs broke loose and chased after it. Then, when Wiley was coming back from the barn with the baby pig in his arms, another animal, big as a horse with a long horn growing from its nose, ran by. Wiley's other dog broke away and tore off after it and disappeared.

Wiley slammed the door of the cabin behind him and shut the latch tight.

"Put the pig in your bed, Wiley, and heap up all the covers on top of it," said his mama.

So Wiley did that, and as he was pulling the covers over the pig, he got a creepy feeling up around the back of his neck. There was a scraping against the wall of the cabin, then a noise of footsteps on the roof, only it didn't sound quite like a person's footsteps.

"Ooooow! That's hot!" the Hairy Man hollered. He started cursing and swearing something fierce, and the whole cabin shook so hard Wiley thought it would fall down around him. Soon there was a knock on the door.

"Quick! Scoot up into the loft where he can't see you," Wiley's mama whispered, and when he was out of sight, she opened the door.

"Mama!" the Hairy Man hollered out. "I done come to get your young 'un."

"Well, you can't have him," said Wiley's mama.

"Then I'll bite you and poison you," he shouted.

"I'll bite you and poison you right back."

"Give him here, or I'll set your house on fire with lightning."

"I've got plenty of sweet milk to put out the fire," said Wiley's mama.

"Give him over, or I'll dry up your spring, make your cow go dry, and send a million boll weevils out of the ground to eat up your cotton."

"Hairy Man, you wouldn't do all that, would you? That's mighty mean."

"I'm a mighty mean man."

"If I give you my baby, will you go on away from here and leave everything else alone and never come back?" Wiley's mama asked.

"I swear that's just what I'll do if you give me your baby."

She opened the door wide and let the Hairy Man into the cabin. "He's over there in that bed," she said.

The Hairy Man crossed over to the bed and snatched off the covers. "Hey!" he hollered. "There ain't nothin' here but a little baby pig!"

"Did I say what kind of baby I was giving you?" asked Wiley's mama. "That pig sure is a baby, and he belonged to me before I gave him to you."

The Hairy Man yelled, gnashed his teeth, and stomped all over the cabin. He grabbed that baby pig and stormed out the door into the swamp, knocking down trees as he ran.

Wiley came down from the loft and looked out the cabin door. It seemed as if a tornado had just passed by. He called and called till his hound dogs were home safe. Then he went inside and grabbed his mama. They sashayed around the cabin and whooped and hollered. "We did it, Mama," said Wiley. "We fooled him three times." As long as they lived—and that was a long, long time—the Hairy Man never did bother Wiley or his mama ever again.

Author's Note

Wiley and the Hairy Man is an Alabama folktale that has become a favorite of storytellers throughout the United States. Tales about a monster who captures children and puts them in a sack are found in many parts of the world. However, tales of an ogre who chases a child up a tree and is frightened off by dogs are uniquely African in origin. In tales from Africa, the ogre has long matted hair and is called Amazimu or Irimu. The Hairy Man is an American confabulation—part European devil, part Amazimu, and part conjure doctor (according to southern folk beliefs, conjure doctors worked with herbs and spells, and had the power to change into animals). I have read and heard many versions of this story, and I've been telling it myself for going on twenty years, so this book is an oral rather than a literary adaptation. Most of the local details and regional expressions in my retelling come from a version, also titled "Wiley and the Hairy Man," collected by Donnell Van de Voort for the Federal Writers' Project of the Works Progress Administration in Alabama.